How to
WEREWOLF

WRITTEN BY MARTIN HOWARD
ILLUSTRATED BY SHOLTO WALKER

Ticktock

An Hachette UK Company
www.hachette.co.uk

First published in Great Britain in 2014 by Ticktock,
an imprint of Octopus Publishing Group Ltd
Endeavour House
189 Shaftesbury Avenue
London
WC2H 8JY
www.octopusbooks.co.uk
www.ticktockbooks.co.uk

ISBN 978 1 84898 927 6

A CIP record for this book is available from the British Library.

Printed and bound in China

1 3 5 7 9 10 8 6 4 2

Project Editor: Catherine Coe   Designer: Hannah Mee
Publisher: Samantha Sweeney   Managing Editor: Karen Rigden
Production Controller: Sarah-Jayne Johnson

Contents

Professor
Van Helsing Phd BA Dip GNVQ
BSC PGCE HND

Chapter 1

WELCOME, YOUNG SLAYER

They call me mad. **MAD!** Me, the great Professor Van Helsing, who has saved the world from Evil more times than you have picked your nose. Me, who has done battle with demons while armed only with a ball of string and my genius! Me, who invented the **Exploding Chicken.**[1]

I am not mad (except on Thursday afternoons). It is all true. All of it! Evil walks and crawls and slithers among us. In the darkness there are teeth, claws and disgusting drooling things with red, **boggly eyes.** The monsters never stop coming, and someone must put up a fight. Admittedly, I am now old. My hair is white and difficult to control. My ears are shrivelled. My knees are creaky and freckled. Once, I could **chase** a werewolf through the darkness all night long, but now I sometimes cannot reach the toilet in time. Even so, I still have my gadgets and a lifetime of experience. Rickety and elderly I may be, but the werewolf that tangles with Van Helsing is a werewolf that's going to wish it had stayed at home, licking its own bottom. Disgusting, **filthy creatures.**

[1] Guaranteed to kill all known werewolves - only £19.99 from the Van Helsing Slayer Supplies and Equipment Company. Free delivery with orders of over £50.

THE MAJESTIC LORD HIGH WIZARD
of the great
UNIVERSITY OF DUMMKOPF
(which is a proper university whatever anyone says)
declares that

Ulrich Viktor Van Helsing

has passed some exam or other.
Possibly. The papers got a bit mixed up. Still, well done him!

He is hereby awarded the title of

PROFESSOR OF DEMONOLOGICAL RESEARCH
*and is now qualified to slay
Creatures of Evil wherever he may find them.*

SIGNED

HIS GRANDNESS, THE MAJESTIC LORD HIGH WIZARD
UNIVERSITY OF DUMMKOPF (A PROPER UNIVERSITY)

In these pages, dear reader, I will impart all my memories, my knowledge and my experience, so that you too can become a slayer. Join me. Not only will you be helping to rid the world of the diabolical forces of Evil, but it's jolly good fun, too. There are people who think that a slayer must be some kind of Chosen One, with special powers or magical weapons. They are wrong. With this book, anyone can be a slayer. Just you wait and see. It is difficult to believe, but even I, the great Van Helsing, was once just an ordinary boy.

"Ha ha," I hear you say, "the legendary Van Helsing - ordinary? It is not possible."

But Van Helsing never lies.

How I Came to Be a Slayer

My story began many years ago, in the small German town of Grüselighausen. Oh the fun I had wading through the swamps, exploring the ruined castles and getting lost in the forests! But that was before Great-Aunt Hellga showed me that the world is infested with Evil.

4

Grüselighausen

She was a quiet woman, **Great-Aunt Hellga** - the sort of great-aunt who knits socks and wears a frilly cap. She was a little hairy, it's true, but great-aunts so often *are* hairy, aren't they? I remember she was always sucking a mint. Her breath smelled so bad it made you want to pull your own nose off.

I thought nothing of this until a creaking floorboard woke me late one night. By the light of the full moon pouring through my bedroom window, I saw a beast creep into my room - a beast that looked like **Great-Aunt Hellga!**

My great-aunt was even hairier than usual – her head, neck and arms were covered in black **fur** – and she was walking on all fours. Her face had... well, the thought of her face still gives me nightmares. Her great mouth was open and **dripping drool** upon the rug. Her teeth were **sharp** and shining in the moonlight. Her snout snuffled as she padded across the floor towards the cage that held my pet hamster. I was **terrified**.

Hardly daring to **breathe**, I did not move or make a sound as she reached into the cage with her horrid claws and grabbed poor, squeaking little **Freddi**.

As I watched her gobble him down in one bite, I knew I would spend the rest of my life **exterminating** monsters like Great-Aunt Hellga. For Freddi.

Poor **Freddi**. I still miss him.

I had a month until the next full moon.
In that time I took my first steps on a path that would lead me to become the world-famous slayer that I am today. I asked

questions: why did the people of Grüselighausen lock themselves inside every night? If no one lived in all the ruined castles, why could I see lights in their windows from my bedroom? Why did such a small town have so many graveyards, and why did so many of the graves have letterboxes?

Slowly, I uncovered the whispered truth: Grüselighausen was not only home to the living but to the ghastly undead too. The town was crawling with Creatures of the Dark. Such as werewolves. Oh, there were lots and lots of werewolves. Great-Aunt Hellga was one of them.

There was one question at the front of my mind: *How do you slay a werewolf?*

The answer to that question, and more, will be revealed within these pages. For now, let me just say that when the full moon rose again Great-Aunt Hellga *mysteriously* vanished. A week later I had a new werewolf-fur hat for the winter. Soon, rumours spread around Grüselighausen. As you can see from this small selection of the many letters I received, I soon became very busy…

Dear Young Master Van Helsing,

They say that you can be trusted.
Please help us! Granny's always been
hairy but now my wife and I are having to shave
her every day, and when we take her out
shopping she pees up against lamp posts
in the street.
The doctor says this is unusual in a woman of
her age (Granny is ninety-four).
Could she be a werewolf?
If so, my wife and I would be ever so grateful
if you could pop round and slay her
when you have a spare moment.

Yours sincerely,
Otto Böring

To the Van Helsing boy,

My husband is a horrid, badly trained beast who drools on
the carpet and keeps scratching at the door to be let out
at night. Please come and put him out of my misery.
Yours,

Grunhilde von Luftwigg

Greetings, young Van Helsing,

All of Grüselighausen is talking of your exploits. They say that you have come to deliver us from the werewolf curse! I would like to shake you by the hand, young man! In the meantime, I thought you might like to know that Horst Dagwurst at 83 Grossbotti Street has a very large beard. Also, he borrowed my lawnmower last week and has not returned it. Surely, the mark of a beast!

Sincerely,

Fritz Bludwurst
82 Grossbotti Street

PS: When you have slain Horst Dagwurst, please return the lawnmower to the shed at the back of my garden.

Van Helsing,

AAAAARGGGHHH!!!!!

IT'S COMING IN THROUGH THE WINDOW.

LOOK AT THE SIZE OF ITS TEETH!

IT'S GOT MY FOOT!!!

HELP! HELP!!!!

Hoping this finds you and your family in excellent health.
I look forward to seeing you at your earliest convenience.

Yours sincerely,
Jürgen Niedöderliebenmunchkin-Lampschade.

lone, I slayed them all. As the years passed, my fame spread. I travelled the world, always seeking out the **monsters** and inventing new and better ways to slay them, such as the *Van Helsing False-Bottom Concrete Fang-Breaker™*.

The Da

"FULL MOON" MURDERS OVER
"MAD" VAN HELSING CLAIMS WEREWOLF SLAIN

POLICE IN THE VILLAGE OF Bishopspiddle have released a statement saying the ghastly murders that shocked the country have stopped. "It's a mystery," said Chief Detective Roger Copper, scratching his head. "We were getting a ghastly murder every night during every full moon until that strange Van Helsing chap showed up. Then they stopped. Just like that. It wasn't anything to do with the police. We were just bumbling about in the dark without a clue. As usual."

The loony Professor Van Helsing, or "Mad Van" as he is usually known, told our reporter Jennifer Kidney, "It was a werewolf. I am NOT mad! Stop writing down that I am mad! I can see you doing it!"

He added, "Once again, the incredible and invincible Va Helsing has saved the day. Woul you like to buy a fur coa Genuine wolf. Only £50."

In the light of day the newspapers called me mad, but when night fell and the moon rose and the **wolves** began howling at the door, people always begged Professor Van Helsing to come.

y Howl

"I am NOT mad," said the professor at Bishopspiddle yesterday.

YOUR TURN TO SLAY

Now, it's *your* turn. **Are you ready?**

Do not be afraid, for with the great **Van Helsing** guiding you, you'll soon be wearing your very own werewolf-fur hat. You must only be brave enough to stare hideous screaming horror in the face and poke it in the eye. Step by step, I will teach you everything you need to know about these fearsome creatures, including spotting a werewolf problem (the blood and **mangled** bodies usually give it away), how to **track** down your **prey** and how to slay it with the minimum amount of fuss and bother. **Slaying** werewolves has never been so easy!

By the time you've finished this book, you'll be exterminating them with absolute confidence. Only **Professor Van Helsing's** amazing advice can make this promise, so do not be fooled by impostors and imitators (especially Doctor Harold Von Dirtfinger's *Werewolf Slaying: A Beginner's Guide*, which is **rubbish**).

Happy slaying,

Chapter 2

INTO THE JAWS OF DEATH

Ha, **young** slayer, I bet you want to get started. Probably already **sharpening** your weapons and thinking you might skip this chapter so you can read the grisly bits, eh? But no - put down that **crossbow** and stop stuffing that chicken with dynamite. You have just started on your journey. Soon, I will teach you how to slay, but first you must learn the truth about **werewolves.**

"But a werewolf is a werewolf is a werewolf," I hear you say. "Big chomping teeth, fur, etc. Stop babbling on, Van."

Wait.

As I always say: an unprepared **slayer** is a *dead* slayer. So **dead** they'll be able to fit what's left of you in a small paper bag. The werewolf, or **Luposapian Horribilis** as we professors call it, is a fearsome beast. Once you see just how fearsome, you may decide to take up knitting instead.

Read on, if you **dare**…

WHAT IS A WEREWOLF?

The word "werewolf" means "man-wolf".[2] Some people think this means that the werewolf is just a **normal**, everyday wolf wearing torn trousers. If this were true, slaying them would be no problem. An old lady could do it with her handbag. In case you're wondering, **werewolves** are also not just normal humans who need flea shampoo, a visit to the dentist and some nail clippers.[3]

In fact, the transformation from human to werewolf is **highly complex**. The werewolf is a mix of different parts of both wolf and human. From the wolf, the werewolf has intelligence, ferocity, speed, stealth, excellent hunting skills and ultra-sharp senses.

[2] The la-di-da scientific word for people who turn from human to wolf is "lycanthrope", but as it's rather a mouthful, even most scientists can't be bothered with it.

[3] Werewolves are also NOT silly old men who like to take all their clothes off, bury bones in the back garden, chase the neighbour's cat and waste a slayer's valuable time. Yes, this means you, Mr Edmund Tiddlington from Barking. You are NOT the "Barking *Wolfman*", you are just barking mad.

From humans it has...ummm...the ability to look like a human (except during the **full moon**) and...errr...that's about it really.

But there is **more**.

Werewolves have strength and **healing powers** far beyond any real wolf or human, as well as an unquenchable thirst for terror and blood and - strangely - chickens. In fact, the werewolf is to a wolf what a great white shark is to a goldfish: they both look like fish but I know which one I would prefer to fight with my bare hands. In the same way, the werewolf might *look* like a huge, mad wolf with burning eyes and great **dripping jaws**, but it is *much*, much worse.

MYTH VERSUS REALITY

There are some things that many people get wrong about werewolves, but the slayer must know the truth...

MYTH 1:
Werewolves Aren't Real

WRONG. Most people go around laughing and jeering and pointing at anyone who thinks **werewolves** really exist. They even call them **"mad"**! Then they act all surprised when they are eaten by one. Werewolves are as real as you and I. Of course, governments keep this information quiet. If the truth were known, everyone would run around screaming and waving their arms in the air. Here are just two of the Top-Secret files I have ~~stolen~~ collected that prove their existence...

F.B.W.
Federal Bureau of Weirdness

TO: Professor Van Helsing
FROM: Harold J. Appliance (Director)

President of the United States of America has turned werewolf. Again. French ambassador eaten. Travel immediately to Washington, D.C. Fake passport and tickets enclosed. Take all necessary action to remove threat. Speak to no one. Usual payment.

Harold J. Appliance

P.E.S.T.
Her Majesty's Department of Protection from
Extraordinary Supernatural Threats

To: ███████████
From: ███████████ ████████

Re: Operation Riding Hood

Dear Prime Minister

Please be notified that P.E.S.T. has identified and confirmed Threat A7GH Alpha. There is a dirty great werewolf on the loose in London!

Gulp.

The attached photograph was taken by Agent

███████ ███████ last night. Please note Big Ben and the Houses of Parliament with a full moon in the background and, of course, the massive werewolf leaping towards the camera. P.E.S.T. will proceed with Operation Riding Hood. We are bringing in Van Helsing.
Yours
███████ ███████

PS: Agent ███████ ███████'s funeral is next Wednesday. ████████

MYTH 2:
Werewolves Only Change When There Is a Full Moon

WRONG. A werewolf can change at any time it chooses, though it has no choice about transforming when the **moon** is full. At this time of the month a few decide to protect their secret by chaining themselves up in a strong cage. Most, however, prefer to simply gobble up anyone who sees them.

MYTH 3:
A Dead Werewolf Turns Back Into a Human

WRONG. A werewolf that is slain in its wolf form stays in its wolf form, which is just as well - it could be tricky for the slayer to explain why they are standing over Auntie Sheila's dead body with a crossbow in hand. Also, very few people want a hat made from Auntie-Sheila skin.

MYTH 4:
Being Bitten by a Werewolf Will Turn You Into One

WRONG. A werewolf never, ever stops at **ONE** bite. What's left of its victim couldn't turn into a were-gerbil. In fact, werewolf blood runs in families, though it is never possible to tell who will be struck by the curse. The affliction may stay hidden for hundreds of years before a werewolf's great-great-great-great-granddaughter suddenly finds herself with a litter of very hairy babies.

How to Spot a Werewolf

The **true horror** of the werewolf is that to the untrained eye, they look just like normal people. Anyone might be a werewolf, as **Little Red Riding Hood**[4] found out. But although the werewolf may look like your **sweet**, rosy-cheeked grandmother who has false teeth and only ever seems to eat biscuits soaked in tea, don't be fooled. Underneath, it will *always* be thinking about chewing on its next victim rather than a soggy custard cream. Most werewolves have learned to hide their secret well, but the mark of the beast cannot be hidden from the keen slayer.

There are many **signs** to look for.

IMPORTANT:
WEREWOLVES WILL KILL TO PROTECT THEIR SECRET.

NEVER SHOW THAT YOU SUSPECT SOMEONE UNTIL YOU ARE READY TO SLAY.

[4] The story of Little Red Riding Hood was rewritten because the true tale was too scary. What actually happened was that the grandmother's teeth were all the better to eat her with. Little Red Riding Hood ended up as lunch while Granny burped happily and had an after-dinner mint.

Hair

Keep an eye out for people with **thick** and **glossy** manes and those who have a lot more body hair than usual. A full beard on a woman is normally a dead giveaway, though, for reasons not yet scientifically understood, female geography teachers also tend to grow thick beards. In addition to hairiness the slayer **MUST** collect extra evidence. Some perfectly normal people - as well as geography teachers - are naturally quite hairy.

The Signs:

Eyebrows that meet in the middle, hairy knuckles, toes and even palms.

People who own a lot of razors, shaving soap, aftershave, hair removal creams, tweezers and - in extreme cases - garden shears.

Anyone who spends a lot of time in the bathroom.

Glove wearers.

VAN'S TIP: Do **NOT** slay someone just because they have shiny hair: they may have just stepped out of the salon.

Ears

The werewolf has extremely sharp hearing and even in human form can hear a **dog whistle** or a **pin drop**. Its ears are always a little more pointed than most humans' and may be hairy even if the rest of the body isn't. Always check closely, especially on cold days. Attacking people who are wearing fur earmuffs can lead to unpleasant misunderstandings.

The Signs:

People who grow their hair over their ears.

Those who whimper and crawl under the bed during firework displays.

People who avoid parks or anywhere dogs are taken for walks.

Anyone who wears a hat at all times.

VAN'S TIP: A dog whistle is the slayer's friend. The sound it makes is too high for humans to hear but not for a werewolf's ears. Blow one and see if anyone looks round. Also try saying "woof" very quietly, and watching for a reaction.

Silver

Werewolves **HATE** silver. It is one of the few things that can kill them. Even the touch of it will make their **skin sizzle** like a frying pan full of bacon. No werewolf will have silver in the house.

The Signs:

Anyone who crosses the road to avoid a jewellery shop.

People who refuse to shake hands if you are wearing a silver ring.

Common excuses include a sudden need to go to the toilet, remembering they left the oven on and pretending they have an infectious skin disease and/or a fear of hands.

Food

Even in human form werewolves find it difficult to resist raw flesh. However, most will have trained themselves to nibble the occasional carrot to disguise their ghastly appetites. Nevertheless, all werewolves would prefer meat for every meal, preferably so raw that it is still moving.

Uncontrollable drooling when passing butchers' shops.

BUTCHERS

The Signs:

Salad dodgers.

Anyone being followed by a pack of dogs (werewolves often have pockets stuffed with raw meat as a mid-morning snack).

VAN'S TIP: Suspect someone is a werewolf but not certain? Serve them a raw steak for lunch and see what happens. Look for growling and sudden hair growth. Be VERY careful - you may be next on the menu.

Breath

Unlike in the fairy tale, a **werewolf** cannot huff and puff and blow your house down, but its **breath** can stink up the place so badly that even pigs will be running for the exits. It is worse when it is in werewolf form but the revolting stench never completely goes away.

The Signs:

Those who talk with one hand covering their mouth.

Plants and flowers withering as someone walks past.

Mint suckers, mouthwash garglers and frequent teeth brushers.

Howling

Few werewolves are **stupid** enough to be caught out this way, but all will have a strong urge to **howl** at the moon even if it is **not** full.

The Signs:

Anyone wearing dark glasses at night.

People who appear jumpy or nervous when the moon is visible. They may also say things like, "Good evening, how ar-ooooooo?"

THE WEREWOLF TRANSFORMATION

The **metamorphosis** of a werewolf is a ghastly process that takes about **three minutes.** It involves a lot of grunting and snarling and some awful smells. It's best to hold your **nose.**

VAN'S TIP: Werewolves are helpless during the early stages of transformation and therefore easy to slay. Though you might be thought of as a bit of a wimp.

STAGE 1

The first thing to change is the werewolf's breath. It is never minty fresh but now it will start to stink like a mixture of old dead things and dirty toilets with a dash of sweaty feet.

STAGE 2

Fingernails quickly grow into sharp claws. Thick, rough fur sprouts all over the body including the face and hands.

STAGE 3

An interesting stage. Halfway through the transformation, the semi-werewolf will drop to all fours, bones cracking as its body changes, and start sniffing its own bottom.
This can be awkward at parties.

STAGE 4

The werewolf will tear off its now too-tight clothes with its new claws. It will drool as its teeth lengthen into fangs. If you value your life this is an excellent moment to run away screaming.

STAGE 5

Known scientifically as the "ugh, that's disgusting" stage, during the final part of the transformation the nose stretches into a muzzle with a painful, wet grinding sound, while the ears prick up, already listening for prey.

KNOW YOUR ENEMY: THE COMPLETE WEREWOLF

So what does the transformed werewolf really look like? All will now be revealed.

MUSCLES

The werewolf has greater strength than any man or wolf. It can run all night, leap over any wall and tear a small building apart in under seven minutes. Imagine what it can do to its victims!

CLAWS

Sharp as razors and as strong as steel, these claws can rip through almost anything, including armour, doors and - as I have found out - even the sturdiest trousers.

EARS

Pointed, large and able to hear an earwig blowing its nose across a desolate moor.

EYES

The werewolf can see in the dark, which is a tiny bit of a pain in the neck for anyone trying to hide.

NOSE

This tippety-toppety nose is super-sensitive (which can be used to your advantage - see Chapter 4). The werewolf can track down a cocktail sausage from twenty miles away.

FACE

In a word: ugly. This is NOT a face you want to see staring through your window in the middle of the night. Some victims die of fright as soon as they see a werewolf. They are the lucky ones.

JAWS AND TEETH

Usually drooling and blood-stained, the werewolf's powerful jaws can bite through steel. It can gobble a large chicken with a single snap of its needle-sharp teeth.

Chapter 3
THE WEREWOLF WORLD

Unfortunately, **werewolves** can be found all over the world. They have spread like **Cousin Olga's** athlete's foot, and come in many shapes and sizes - all of them more ghastly than a hat full of scorpions. The horrible creatures have adapted to live in most places and are found everywhere.

I have hunted great shaggy werewolves in the mountain villages of the **Himalayas** and *been* hunted by sleek, deadly Nagual werewolves in the jungles of South America. What you need to remember is: the wise slayer knows everything about their prey. Knowing your **Mexican** Nagual from your melancholy **Swedish** werewolf might mean the difference between life and death.

WHERE DO WEREWOLVES COME FROM?

How and when the first werewolf appeared is something of a mystery, even to me. Nevertheless, I have a theory: Long, long ago, when humans were more grunty, they decided the noble wolf would be a suitable pet.[5] This meant that over hundreds of years wolves changed from intelligent, strong, **silent night hunters** into little yappy fluff-balls begging for scraps, chasing sticks and wearing collars and ribbons in their hair.

The real wolves that remained saw their brothers and sisters begging from the table and licking faces, and became very angry. In **revenge**, they took small children (this is why there are so many old stories about children being raised by wolves) and began changing them. Humans had turned wolves into dogs, and now wolves created **wolf-humans**, keeping them in their wild world for so long that the children grew hairy and powerful and deadly. Then they sent them back to hunt. The werewolf had been **born!**

[5] Woolly mammoths were tried first, but quickly discarded when they started trying to curl up on their owners' laps in the evenings.

There are of course other theories about how **werewolves** first came into being. For many years I have enjoyed collecting them as part of my library.

Take a look at this piece for example:

I found this **Ancient Egyptian** papyrus while hunting down a werewolf in the **tombs** and pyramids of **Cairo**. It shows the wolf-headed god Fi-Do laying a curse on a man who had stolen the god's bone of power. The curse turned the thief into the first werewolf. It was later killed by a slayer whose name – if my translation of the ancient hieroglyphics is correct – was **Vanhelsis the Mighty.**

And there's this **old parchment** which I discovered in the library of the **University of Dummköpf** and forgot to take back.[6]

Hark ye to this warning and beware the beast that has killed. It hunts me. Through the night, every night, it hunts me.

My people made the mistake of making war upon a tribe called the Lunatix. We slayed them all, or thought we did, but our chief was killed in battle. His only son, Ethelred the Flower-Arranger, become our new chief. Instead of battle and glory, Ethelred preferred long walks in the country and baking cakes. We begged the gods to make him strong and fierce like his father. The gods answered – a druid came to our village. One stormy night, beneath a full moon, this mysterious spell-weaver sacrificed a wolf and performed a powerful ritual of dark magic.

Afterwards, Ethelred seemed no different, but the druid told us to wait.

At the next full moon, Ethelred the Flower-Arranger became Ethelred the Wolf. No longer did he want cake.

I and the druid escaped his terrifying

the druid had gone I found a note fr

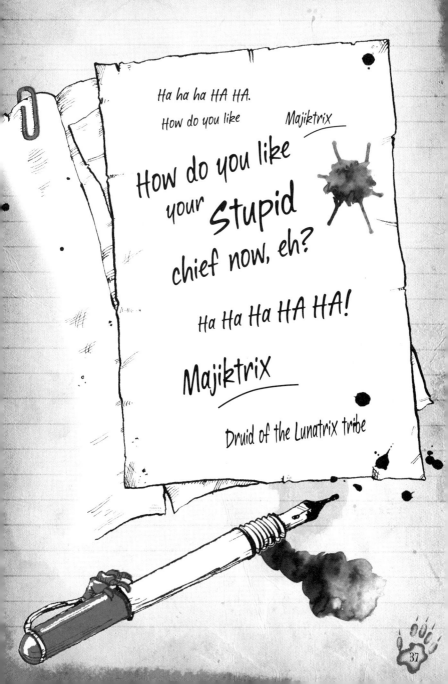

Werewolves of the Past

However the werewolf first came into existence, we know one thing for sure: throughout history there have been many recorded outbreaks, and – I am proud to say – the **Van Helsing family** has always been on hand to help. You are in safe hands, dear reader, just look at the evidence...

A letter sent by my great-great-great-great-aunt **Grünhilde** from Poligny in France.

My dearest darling Horst,

What a dreadful time it has been for a feeble and frail woman like your poor Grünhilde! I declare, travelling these terrible roads has left me as tired and weak as a kitten. And then, a werewolf attack. And I was wearing my new dress!

The horrible, horrible creature sprang at me with hunger in its glowing red eyes – just like old Johann Bümfur at the Winter Ball last year. Then it put one of its nasty dirty paws on my dress. I'm afraid your sweet, timid little Grünhilde became quite cross. I punched the ghastly thing in the throat, then broke its knee with a tiny kicky-wicky.

As it lay there howling, I jumped up and down on its head. Not very ladylike, I know, but silk is soooo very difficult to get clean.

Your loving
Grünhilde

August, 1521

VAN'S NOTE: I have seen portraits of Great-Aunt Grünhilde. She was the size of a small building and could carry a cow under each arm.

Then there was the infestation of werewolves in the German town of Griefswald in 1640.

This page comes from my great-great-great-grandfather's diary.

Journal of Munter Van Helsing

November 16th, 1640

Arrived in the town of Griefswald. Disgusting wolf vermin haunt every street and alleyway. No citizen is safe. Why, I had to slay three just getting from my carriage to the inn! Slayed two more of the pestilential beasts howling beneath my window. How is a man to sleep?

November 17th, 1640

Once again the immense Van Helsing brain has found a solution. I asked the people of Griefswald to bring me every scrap of silver within the town. Luckily, I brought Wolfshredding Wanda, my trusty gun. Today, we made bullets. Tonight I hunt. Received a letter from Agnes. Her ankles are playing up again.

November 18th, 1640

I have returned home. Griefswald is clean of wolves. (Note: the line "Well, that was another howling success," after I had killed the beasts caused many admiring laughs – use again.) What remained of the silver seems to have accidentally fallen into my luggage. Carriage jingles!

What's this? Oh, yes, a page from "Gibbering" Olaf Van Helsing's notebook.

London, May 5th, 1725

Ah ha! They said I was mad, but I have discovered the werewolf's greatest weakness! It is cheese! It burns them. Oh, how it burns them. I have built a giant trap made entirely of cheese and made myself weapons of cheese. Now it comes.

It is here! It has entered the trap.

Oh.

We don't talk about **Uncle Olaf** much but family legends say he wasn't really a Van Helsing at all. The story goes that he was found as a baby in the smoking remains of a mad **scientist's** castle. The Van Helsings adopted him, but he never really got the hang of the family business.

THE WORLD OF WOLVES

Unfortunately, there are very few corners of the world that are free of the werewolf curse and the slayer's work is never done. They're like the washing up - just when you think you've finished them all off, they start piling up again, and they only get worse the longer you leave them. Slay one in **Italy** and two will pop up in **Tasmania**. Clean up **London** and an infestation will break out in **Paris**.

There are many different kinds and the slayer who wants to stay alive will be familiar with all of them. Here's what you need to know:

KITSUNE

(say: kit-soo-nay)

Found in Japan and China, Kitsune are more were *foxes* – they are born foxes and turn into humans. They are more attractive than proper werewolves (what isn't?), smaller and can be vicious. Myths say they grow up to nine tails though I have never met a Kitsune with more than one. This is a shame as their tails make excellent dusters.

HOW TO SPOT A KITSUNE

- Like normal werewolves, Kitsune in human form are unusually hairy, though sleeker, and have white patches.

- Look for a fox-shaped shadow, or a foxy reflection in mirrors. Or a funny-looking lump in the back of their trousers: Kitsune don't always lose their tails when they take human form.

- Kitsune hate dogs, so always carry a Chihuahua in your pocket.

SLAYING A KITSUNE

Kitsune like to play cruel tricks on their victims rather than just eating them straight away. You can easily put a stop to this with a large axe.

LOBISÓN
(say: low-bee-son)

A particularly repulsive-looking creature with great hunched shoulders and, often, a large moustache, the Lobisón can be found across Argentina and Brazil. The Lobisón mostly eats dead things, giving it the worst breath of any werewolf. I have only slayed one and that was a difficult hunt, mainly because it is impossible to get within thirty metres of the beast without fainting from the stench. I had to sneak up on it in a hot-air balloon.

HOW TO SPOT A LOBISÓN

• Most of the normal rules apply, but the Lobisón likes the taste of rotting meat in particular. Keep a sharp eye out for people who lurk around the bins behind restaurants.

• The Lobisón often hangs about in graveyards. Be careful how you slay: that group of people wearing black might just be there to bury Granddad.

SLAYING A LOBISÓN

Keep upwind and use *very* long-range weapons, a rifle or a guided missile if you have one.

LOUP GAROU
(say: loop gar-oooo)

Ooh la la! The Loup Garou is a French werewolf and similar to the classic werewolf, except for one or two small differences. In wolf form, the Loup Garou will eat as many as five or six people in one night, plus a cheese course. After turning back into a human it will be weak and faint for some time. It also burps frequently.

HOW TO SPOT A LOUP GAROU

- Loup Garous have bristles beneath their tongues. One way of checking is to kiss them, but this is NOT recommended: you may lose your lips. Disguise yourself as a dentist instead.
- Look out for anyone who looks as if they have eaten too much the night before and is grumpy in the mornings, although, in France, this means almost everyone.

SLAYING A LOUP GAROU

If you know the name your werewolf uses when human, the Loup Garou can be cured by saying it three times to its wolf form, while striking it gently on the head with a knife. I have found that keeping quiet and striking it extremely hard on the head with a large axe works just as well.

NAGUAL

(say: na-wall)

The Mexican werewolf is a peculiar beast. As I found out (by losing the tip of an ear), silver has no effect on them, which makes slaying much less expensive. Legends say that the Nagual is a witch or sorcerer who is able to change themself into the form of any animal: wolf, jaguar, monkey, owl, stick insect, etc. This is perplexing. As far as I know, no one has ever had their throat ripped out by a were-stick insect, but stranger things have happened.[7]

HOW TO SPOT A NAGUAL

• The Nagual witch or sorcerer transforms into a beast only during the night while sleeping. If you see anyone sleeping at night, add them to your list of highly suspicious characters.

• A few Naguals are proud of their ability and don't even *try* to keep their grisly secret. It's worth asking everyone you meet, "Hey, are you a disgusting fiend that stalks the night as a beast?"

SLAYING A NAGUAL

Any normal weapon will slay a Nagual, plus fire, holy water and stones. If you meet a Nagual who has transformed into a slug you can just step on them.

[7] I was once attacked by a possessed carpet.

SKIN WALKER

The North American Skin Walker terrorises Native Americans and is a magical human who can change into any animal it likes, though the wolf form is a favourite.

It is also able to transform into other people, which the Navajo Indians call "face stealing".

Unfortunately, it is also very good at arm stealing, leg stealing and head stealing. These horrors like to cast evil spells, using tarantulas, rattlesnakes and squirrels in their foul magics.

HOW TO SPOT A SKIN WALKER

• Skin Walkers have a yellow tinge to their skin which, thankfully, makes them easy to spot. They will try to disguise this so be suspicious of anyone with a bag on their head.
• Look out for those who carry spiders, snakes and squirrels in their handbag.

SLAYING A SKIN WALKER

Only a bullet covered in white ash will slay a Skin Walker, so keep a pocketful of ash handy.

EIGI EINHAMR
(say: eye-gee ein-hamma)

Meaning "not of one skin", the Eigi Einhamr can be found in Norway, Sweden and Denmark and is said to transform into a werewolf when it wears the skin of a wolf. This is complete rubbish! I own several wolfskin hats, a wolfskin coat, as well as wolfskin trousers, gloves and underwear, and I have never turned into a wolf.

In fact, the Eigi Einhamrs are just common werewolves trying to be different and can be spotted and slain as normal. They are miserable creatures who like nothing better than a good moan. Typical. With werewolves it's all about me, me, me. Slaying them soon puts them out of everyone's misery.

Canadian werewolves are a peculiar mix of Loup Garou and the common European werewolf. Unusually friendly and polite, they make their victims feel comfortable and welcome before eating them.

Greenland

Canada

Werewolves in Greenland are protected by their thick fur coats and don't mind the cold. They do get sick of eating polar bears all the time though.

USA

Af

South America is heaving with werewolves, and they have many different names. Some of them – like Tlahuelpuchi – are so difficult to pronounce that people have been known to choke to death while trying to scream, "Help, help, I'm being attacked by a Tlahuelpuchi."

Brazil

Argentina

There is evidence that werewolves originated in Africa, but the whole continent is mysteriously free of them now. Some people think this is due to some work of great magic by African slayers in the past. Others think it is because elephants sat on them all.

Russia

China

Werewolves avoid India as the victims available there are "too spicy" for their tastes.

There are very few Australian werewolves, mainly because any creature running around at night with no shoes on is almost certainly going to step on a poisonous snake or insect, or a crocodile.

Australia

Chapter 4
THE COMPLETE SLAYER

Now, it is time to learn how to fight your enemy! Soon, you too can be a world-saving hero like me: bold, dashing and just a little bit fearsome. Of course, being a **slayer** is not just a job, it is a *lifestyle*. You will be always on duty, ready to step in when peril threatens and danger rears its repulsive, drooling head.

You're sure you want to be a slayer? It is not yet too late. You can still put this book down and take up a job that is less **dangerous** - lion-taming or tiger-juggling perhaps.

If you're sure, many changes await you. Look how I changed from a **spotty lad** in embarrassing leather shorts to a slaying **hero**. Those were the days: up at sunrise, running through the forests of Grüselighausen to improve my stamina, lifting weights to improve my strength and hunting to improve my...err...hunting. Quickly, I grew fit. My muscles bulged. My teeth twinkled. The young women of Grüselighausen swooned when they saw me and the men all wished to shake my hand.

I learned many valuable lessons in those days.

The first was the most important. The werewolf curse still hung heavy upon the town. Soon, I was ready to slay my second beast: **Herman Schnausermann**, the local bank manager.

He was a small man with a bristly moustache, hairy legs and a twitchy eye. I had long suspected him of being a werewolf. Several of the bank's customers had gone missing, and I had once seen him scratching his ear. "That's not unusual," you may say. "I scratch my ear all the time." Yes, but do you do it with your toes?

When the full moon arrived, I took an axe and waited outside the bank. Later, as I lay in bed with thirteen broken bones, a cracked skull, torn muscles, blood pouring from a dozen wounds and a terrible case of fleas, I had plenty of time to think about that first valuable lesson. The lesson was this: jogging around the woods and doing a few push-ups does **NOT** make you a slayer. I had been lucky with **Great-Aunt Hellga**, but there was more work to do before I could slay **Herman Schnausermann**.[8]

[8] I learned my lesson well. Next time I saw him it was through the crosshairs of a very long-range crossbow.

What to Wear

Now we begin the most important part of your transformation into a slayer, starting with style...

"**Huh?**" you may say. "What does style matter to a slayer? Who cares what you wear so long as the job gets done?" This is nonsense. As I found out on that long-ago day in Grüselighausen, the successful slayer cannot face their enemy wearing leather shorts that have grown far too small.

Neither can they say things like "Ummm...good evening, Mr Schnausermann, sir. I've...errr...come to...ummm...slay you. If you don't mind. **Thankyousoverymuch**." The werewolf simply chuckles under its breath while it watches its **claws** growing and glinting in the moonlight. And the slayer begins shaking and spluttering things like, "**Or** we could l-leave it u-until **t-t-tomorrow** if it's **i-inconvenient**. Should I make an appointment with your **s-s-secretary?**"

No, it is important that the werewolf is more terrified of you than you are of it. This means facing it with a certain style: dressed to impress, a wink in your eye and a clever put-down on your lips. The werewolf is used to its victims **screaming**, **blubbering** and tearing their own hair out with fear. An enemy who looks and acts as cool as a fridge full of **cucumbers** will confuse and frighten it.

The slayer will need to feel at home in many places – from stately homes and the **Prime Minister's office** to misty, desolate moors. With a little thought it is possible to be combat-ready while always looking confident and stylish. The look you are aiming for is **noble hero**.

VAN'S TIP: Pockets, pockets, pockets! Remember: weapons, maps, traps and gizmos are all part of the slayer's inventory. You can never have too many pockets.

HAT: A knitted woollen hat might be nice and warm, but does it say "slayer"? No. Try something with a wide brim that can be pulled over the eyes. This can be a useful disguise and makes any slayer look dashingly mysterious.

VAN'S TIP: Black is good for camouflage and never goes out of fashion.

COAT: A long, black leather coat offers warmth and protection and can hide numerous useful pockets. Most importantly, it looks fabulous when you are standing in the moonlight, crossbow in hand, with the wind billowing it out behind you. A must-have for any serious slayer.

UNDERWEAR: For outdoor hunting wear warm underwear. Also bear in mind that your clothes may be shredded by a werewolf's claws and teeth during that desperate fight to the death. It is difficult to look heroic when everyone can see you are wearing yesterday's underwear with little love hearts all over them.

JEWELLERY: Silver, obviously. I recommend that every slayer wears at least three or four rings. They're stylish and will cause any werewolf a massive amount of pain when you punch it in the face.

BOOTS: Some suppliers offer boots with hidden blades that spring out of the toecap. I have found these can go off by accident, tripping you up at awkward moments and – on one occasion – cutting off Lady Tuttlington's big toe during an energetic foxtrot at her Grand Summer Ball.

TALKING TO YOUR PREY

There is a saying among slayers: "Speak softly and carry a large axe, sword, crossbow, an assortment of guns, traps, explosives and a **Hungarian gouging spoon.**" When facing your prey you should always be ready with a few sharp, well-chosen words. This will show the werewolf that you are **unafraid.** Also, anyone watching will think you are the bee's knees.

Feel free to make up your own, but here are a few phrases I have used with great success.

"Yes, I *get* it: growl drool snarl snarl howl snuffle howl. *Boring!*"
Roll your eyes and yawn while saying this. Then shoot.

"Down, boy!"
Works well just before slaying. Also, "Bad boy! In your basket!"

"Fetch *this.*"
As you fire a silver-tipped crossbow bolt.

"Looks like someone forgot to shave this morning. Let's see what we can do about that."
Say this as you draw your sword.

"My, what big teeth you have. Feel like picking them up off the floor?"
Follow this with a punch in the mouth.

VAN'S TIP: When talking to your prey, try to stand with the full moon or a burning building directly behind you. It won't make any difference to the werewolf's sharp eyes but you will look unbelievably nifty.

EQUIPMENT AND WEAPONS

The best way to slay a werewolf is from a very, *very* long way away: sitting in a tree with a flask of hot chocolate and a bun if you can. That isn't always possible though, and the slayer should be expert with every kind of weapon. As you advance you will discover which weapons, traps and gizmos suit you best, but the basic slayer inventory should include the following:

COMPASS AND MAP

Always have these about you and learn how to use them! A slayer who wanders around lost on the desolate moor while the werewolf terrorises a village ten miles away is a slayer who will be laughed out of town.

TELESCOPE/BINOCULARS

Werewolves have incredible eyesight; *you* have gadgets. Use them.

SWORD

Werewolves may be difficult to harm with normal weapons and may heal amazingly fast, but even with its supernatural powers any werewolf will find the loss of its head a major inconvenience.

AXE

The traditional tool for killing wolves, as approved by woodchoppers everywhere. All werewolves know this and will be terrified by the sight of a swinging axe. Plus you can chop wood with it - very handy.

SILVER BULLETS

Guns are effective weapons but silver bullets aren't cheap, so keep cost at the front of your mind as that huge, screaming fiend leaps at you from the darkness.

CROSSBOW

There are many crossbows on sale. Find one that is easy to carry, accurate and powerful. Pay attention to styling: a good crossbow should be both a deadly weapon and a natty accessory. Anyone watching should be left gasping in awe as you expertly drop a werewolf with a cool flick of the trigger.

Crossbow bolts should be tipped with silver and, again, this can get expensive. However, they can be easily found after you have slain your prey and reused: doing this with bullets can be messy.

FLAMING TORCH

As waved by many an angry villager, a flaming torch is a useful weapon. Werewolves don't particularly like fire, and for one good reason: their fur is very greasy. Touch a werewolf with a flaming torch and it will go up like a witch on a bonfire.

SILVER-PLATED POCKET/BOOT/SLEEVE DAGGERS

Keep a selection of secret daggers about your person for hand-to-claw fighting and throwing. They are very handy for those "Ooops, I've dropped my weapon," moments.

EXPLOSIVES

No slayer should venture out without Van Helsing's "Chewy Surprise" doggie treats and a stick of dynamite. Remember to bring a box of matches too: trying to light a fuse by rubbing two twigs together while a werewolf is charging at you can be annoying.

Traps and Gizmos

Always have a few surprises up your sleeve. There are many **gizmos** available, including super-powered sirens that will burst any werewolf's sensitive ear drums and wolf-hypnotising sausages. Traps can range from pocket-sized gadgets to **enormous contraptions**. Each has its place in the slayer's kit. Setting up an elaborate trap with tripwires, explosives and sharpened stakes can take time but the end result will be worth it, and watching the werewolf walk into it will make a jolly night out for local children. Simple traps that should be carried at all times include...

Caltrops

These cheeky little gizmos are made of four sharp silver spikes. However you throw them, one spike will always land pointing upwards, just waiting for a werewolf to step on it. You'll hear it screaming from the other side of the desolate moor!

The Boulder

Find a heavy boulder and balance it on the edge of a cliff or steep hill with just a small wedge keeping it in place. (Note: you may need to pay someone to help with this - make sure you add the expense to your bill.)

Attach a long piece of string to the wedge. Mark the spot where the boulder will fall then leap around yelling, "Helloooo, tasty flesh right here. Come and get your tasty flesh, Mr Hairy." When the werewolf reaches the spot you have marked, pull the string. You should now have an extremely flat werewolf. Job done.

Bear Traps

A single bear trap won't slow a werewolf down for long but I have had good results from using twenty at a time.

The Exploding Chicken

Werewolves can't resist a plump, tasty hen so why not serve one with extra spicy stuffing? A high quality exploding chicken (such as those sold by the Van Helsing Slayer Supplies and Equipment Company) will look and smell just like the real thing and will definitely leave a nasty taste in the mouth. They'll be scraping werewolf off the walls five miles away!

The Wolf Mangler

For the slayer who likes to avoid close combat, try the Van Helsing Wolf Mangler featuring FootPad technology.

When the werewolf steps on it a heavy cage drops from above, but that's just the start of the werewolf's problems: the cage is electrified. As your werewolf yelps and crackles, the crushing mechanism is triggered, squashing your werewolf into a small cube. Finally, a small drawer pops out, presenting its remains in a stylish and eye-catching pot, ready for your trophy room or mantelpiece.

VAN'S TIP: Do NOT use the Wolf Mangler in built-up areas.

Check the **Van Helsing Slayer Supplies and Equipment Company** catalogue for all the latest in fun and exciting gadgets at low, low prices - you'll wonder how we do it!

TRAINING

No matter how brave you are and how cool you look, a flabby, out-of-shape slayer is just a werewolf snack on two legs. However, training to slay these beasts can be tricky. Unless you are lucky enough to have a werewolf **trapped** in the cellar, you can't practise fighting and there is no way to prepare for that moment when you first come **face-to-hideous-face** with one. Even so, your life will depend on your slayer skills and you should take every opportunity to keep them sharp. For instance, during breakfast I stick a picture of a werewolf to the wall and throw butter at it. I also like to lurk by the front door and bring the postman down armed with just a slice of toast.

Here's an example training programme, taken straight from my own journal:

4.30 am – 6.00 am: Healthy breakfast, bath, hairstyling and dressing.

6.00 am – 7.00 am: Run, then hiding practice, followed by running and hiding practice.

7.00 am – 9.00 am: Stealth, camouflage and hunting – sneaking, tracking, ducking behind things, general snooping around.

9.00 am – 11.00 am: Target practice – throwing daggers, throwing axes, bow, crossbow, bombs and small cannons.

11.00 am – 12.00 noon: Dealing with complaining neighbours, rebuilding the shed.

12.00 noon – 1.00 pm: Light lunch, hairstyling and wardrobe maintenance.

1.00 pm – 3.00 pm: Strength training – weightlifting, wagon pulling, pig tossing.

3.00 pm – 5.00 pm: Weapons practice – with sword, dagger, spear, etc.

5.00 pm – 6.00 pm: Bandaging.

6.00pm – 8.00pm: Bear hunting followed by hand-to-hand combat training, with bears.

8.00 pm – 9.00 pm: A good dinner of bear stew.

9.00 pm – 12.00 midnight: Night stalking, navigating by the moon training, looking great by moonlight practice.

12.00 midnight: Hairstyling and bed.

UNARMED COMBAT

My advice about fighting with a werewolf without weapons is simple: **NEVER** fight a werewolf without any weapons. Nevertheless, there will be times when even the best prepared slayer will be forced to battle hand to claw. For these times, I have developed a fighting technique I call Van-jit-su. Practise daily, asking friends and family to be your opponent, or simply poke a gorilla with a stick until it attacks you. A complete course can be found in my excellent book, *Van-jit-su Made Easy,* available from the Van Helsing Slayer Supplies and Equipment Company.

The Origami Werewolf

This move is **simple** but **effective** and will leave the werewolf completely knotted.

1 As the werewolf leaps at you, grab it by its ears (remember to wash your hands later).

2 Pull down sharply so that its head is between its legs.

3 Reach down with one hand and pull its rear right paw up behind its neck (be careful of those claws!). Repeat with rear left paw.

4 Taking its front right paw, insert into slot **A** (see diagram). Insert front left paw into slot **B**.

5 Your werewolf should now be in an "oven-ready chicken" position - unable to move and easy to slay.

The Striking Cobra

So, the **werewolf** has you pinned to the ground. **Drool** is **dripping** onto your face and it is just about to sink its **fangs** into your **throat**. Things don't look good but, in fact, you now have the **creature** at your **mercy**.

1 As the werewolf lowers its head to bite you, howling in triumph, bite its nose as hard as you can.

2 The werewolf's howl of triumph will quickly turn into a yelp of pain. Good. Do not let go. This is a great time to use one of those witty slayer phrases. I suggest, "Oo din smell at oming, id oo?"

3 As the werewolf rears back it will leave its nose between your teeth, and hop about the place in pain. You can now slay at your leisure. Remember to use lots of mouthwash later!

The Tail Spin

No animal likes having its tail pulled and werewolves are no different. You will need strength and nerves of concrete for this move but it's a **doozy**. The werewolf will be dazed, hurt and left feeling a bit silly.

1 When the werewolf makes a lunge at you, dive between its legs, roll and come to your feet behind it.

2 Quickly, grab it by the tail. (Note: if you are practising with a friend or family member ask them to tie a length of rope to their belt. **Do NOT** practise this move with the elderly or pets – slayers don't swing old people and kitties around, no matter how grumpy or annoying they might be.)

3 Keeping a tight grip and using all your strength, begin swinging it around in circles. At this point it will be helpless, wondering if attacking a slayer was a very good idea and hoping that none of the other werewolves find out.

4 When the werewolf is spinning at a good speed, let go, preferably close to a wall or a large tree.

5 The beast will smash into the wall/tree head first. It will be stunned, allowing you to slay as and when you feel like it.

The Screaming "Van" Dash

This is one of my **favourite moves** and should be practised every day. It has saved my life more times than I can count.

1 Point yourself in a direction away from the werewolf.

2 Move your legs in a pistoning motion as fast as you possibly can. Move **forward**, avoiding objects in your path. Try to imagine what will happen if the werewolf catches up with you - this will help you go faster.

3 Flap your hands above your head while screaming, **"WAAAAAAAAHHH!"**

4 Continue until you are far, far away from the werewolf.

Dos and Don'ts
for the New Slayer

Here's a handy checklist that you can cut out and keep with you at all times...

DO

- Remember: training, training, training!
- Make sure your hair is looking good and your boots are polished. There's no excuse for sloppiness.
- Change your underwear frequently. You never know!
- Use plenty of deodorant. A werewolf can smell fear.
- Learn how to raise one eyebrow at times of great danger: it looks great.
- Be careful. No matter how confident you are the werewolf is *always* a dangerous foe.
- Keep in mind that the werewolf is also hunting *you.* Keep one or two hidden weapons on you at all times, even in the bath.
- Be creative: everyday household items can be deadly in the right hands. I once slayed a werewolf with a stapler and a dish mop.
- Spend some time each day thinking up witty remarks.
- Enjoy yourself. Just because you are the only thing that stands between humanity and these terrifying creatures doesn't mean you can't smile.

DON'T

- Get too clever. Why make a complicated plan involving kegs of gunpowder, candlelight, a hunchbacked assistant called Igor and a small goat, if a simple crossbow bolt will do?

- Wear leather shorts. *Ever*.

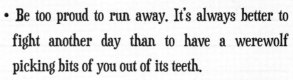

- Be too proud to run away. It's always better to fight another day than to have a werewolf picking bits of you out of its teeth.

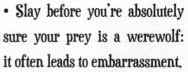

- Slay before you're absolutely sure your prey is a werewolf: it often leads to embarrassment.

- Talk too much. One witty remark is worth more than any amount of nervous blabbering.

- Use weapons you haven't practised with. At best you'll just look silly, at worst you'll cut your own elbows off.

- Give up: the slayer *always* gets their prey.

- Forget to collect your reward.

Chapter 5

THE STRATEGY OF SLAYING

Slaying can be a tricky business, and the slayer who doesn't use their brain is a slayer who will be wiped off the walls with a damp sponge.

However much you might want to, you cannot just walk up to someone and shoot him or her between the eyes with a **silver bullet**, no matter how large his or her moustache is.

As discussed earlier – and this is important – they might **NOT** be a werewolf, and people can be funny about that sort of thing. Secondly, if they are a werewolf, they will probably tear your arm off before you can pull the trigger. No, the slayer must always remember the two Ps: proof and planning. It may seem like a lot of unnecessary fuss and bother, but you must prove a werewolf is a werewolf and form a plan to deal with it quickly and professionally. Then you can move on to the one **D: death** – preferably the werewolf's.

VAN'S TIP: Try to avoid dying (unless it is part of a fiendishly clever plan). Death can slow even the best slayer down and I should know, I have been pronounced dead three times. It stings a bit.

Finding a Werewolf

Werewolves are very good at staying hidden and making sure that no one who sees them lives to tell the tale. Finding one of these foul beasts can be like finding a burp in a hurricane. Once you have become a celebrity slayer like me, people will go down on their knees begging for your services. Until then you'll have to go and find your own werewolves. There are two ways to do this.

Newspapers

Newspapers are the slayer's friend. Circle the dates of the full moon on your calendar and be on the lookout for stories of people disappearing or being horribly murdered immediately after those dates. The alert slayer may find other clues in the story, too. Look at this example...

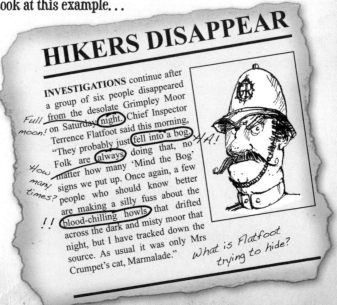

HIKERS DISAPPEAR

INVESTIGATIONS continue after a group of six people disappeared from the desolate Grimpley Moor on Saturday night. Chief Inspector Terrence Flatfoot said this morning, "They probably just fell into a bog. Folk are always doing that, no matter how many 'Mind the Bog' signs we put up. Once again, a few people who should know better are making a silly fuss about the blood-chilling howls that drifted across the dark and misty moor that night, but I have tracked down the source. As usual it was only Mrs Crumpet's cat, Marmalade."

Full moon!

How many times?

!! HA!

What is Flatfoot trying to hide?

I did some quick research to find that over the past ten years more than **600** people had "fallen into a bog" on Grimpley Moor, including everyone who complained about howling. Mrs Crumpet's cat, Marmalade, had died three years before. The culprit was, of course, a werewolf - none other than **Chief Inspector Terrence Flatfoot.**

ADVERTISING

As we have seen, few people believe that werewolves exist. Luckily for the slayer, however, they quickly start believing when one is snuffling at their front door. Anyone who has woken up to the sound of a spine-tingling howl or heard the blood-chilling screams of a werewolf's victims will soon forget that werewolves are made-up beasts and be desperate to find a slayer. You can make it easier for them to find you by placing adverts in shop windows, newspapers, etc.

Paws in the Dirt

So, you've spotted signs of a werewolf infestation in the newspaper, or some terrified citizen has begged for your help, but how do you track your prey down? For such a large and smelly beast, the werewolf can be difficult to locate. It moves through the night as quickly and silently as a well-oiled weasel and its **supernatural senses** of smell and sight means it can easily detect if it is being followed. Once that happens, you might as well smear yourself with tomato ketchup. However, hunting is an unavoidable part of the slayer's job.

CAMOUFLAGE: By wearing black, the slayer should already be well camouflaged during night-time missions. However, this will not stop the werewolf smelling you. To disguise your scent, roll around in muck and cowpats and leaves until you smell like the countryside. (If you are in the city, roll around in the gutter.) Horrible things will stick to your clothes. Your hairstyle will suffer. You will find things crawling out of your ears for days afterwards. Sometimes being a slayer comes at a terrible price.

SPEED AND STEALTH: Moving quickly and silently should be part of every slayer's daily training. You are aiming to be as silent as a ghost.[9] Avoid twigs snapping beneath your feet and pay attention to your breathing - the werewolf will hear you if you start panting like a vampire in a garlic factory. Do NOT swear loudly when you fall into a stream.

PRINTS: Werewolves may slip through the night with cunning stealth but they are large, heavy beasts and will leave a trail of paw prints (and drool and blood) that can be followed by the sharp-eyed slayer.

[9] Not the kind of ghost that throws things around and screams "GETT OOOOOOUUUT" in people's faces when they move into a new house. The kind of ghost that glides silently through walls and wafts up to unsuspecting slayers while they are having their bedtime cocoa, making them spill it all down their pyjamas.

HIDING (IN THE COUNTRY):

Chasing a werewolf across country can very quickly become being chased by a werewolf across country. If that happens, hide. I've lost count of the times I have sat at the bottom of a slimy pond breathing through a reed, and can also recommend tree climbing and wriggling down rabbit holes. If you are lucky, you might later be able to leap out at the surprised werewolf shouting, "Coming, ready or not," as you take aim.

In the City

Like most other supernatural creatures, werewolves have adapted to live in the city. This presents the slayer with problems. Firstly, the slayer will not be able to follow paw prints over cobblestones and pavements. Secondly, the werewolf will avoid crowds and travel through sewers, often making its secret lair in some stinking and forgotten underground hole. Some slayers may wish to follow their prey down a pipe filled with disgusting ooze, but they are on their own. My advice is to throw a couple of smoke bombs in the hole and wait until the werewolf surfaces.

80

Planning and Tactics

Once you have found your werewolf, simply running at it swinging a huge axe and screaming **"AAAAAARGGHHH!"** is a certain way to end up in bite-sized chunks (it also looks silly). The successful slayer outsmarts the cunning werewolf. This means using your brain as well as your axe. Form your plan carefully, **paying attention** to every detail, and the battle is half won before it begins.

Secrecy

It is important to operate in complete secrecy. If the werewolf knows that it's being trailed by a slayer it will be on its guard. Always have a variety of false noses and false identities to hand. The werewolf will take a keen interest in strangers, especially if they look threatening and/or tasty, so try to appear harmless as well as unappetising. I often arrive in a werewolf-infested village dressed as a one-legged tramp (fewer legs for the werewolf to eat) or a big-nosed travelling washerwoman called Madame Winkleblötter, who looks so old and smelly that a werewolf would rather eat its own head than hers.

Maps and Charts

Whether it is a ruined castle, swamp or stately home, always draw plans of your **battleground**. Pay special attention to places where you might wish to ambush the werewolf, marking any traps you set. Make sure that you show these to any confirmed non-werewolf who may be wandering around. **Secrecy** is all very well but I once had to scrape up the Count of Bavaria after he accidentally stepped in one of my **traps**. Annoyingly, this gave the werewolf time to **escape**.

Choosing a Battleground

The time has come to face the beast, and it is important that you choose your position well. Here are a few things to consider.

1. *Can I block the entrance and booby-trap any of the werewolf's escape routes?* There's no point in luring a werewolf if it can just wander off whenever it feels like it.

2. *Do I have at least two escape routes?* You can soon be a long way away with a nice cup of tea and a slice of pie.

3. *Am I out of reach of the werewolf's claws/fangs?* [10] Remember: going hand to claw with a werewolf = bad, shooting at it from a safe distance = good.

4. *How many traps can I lay between me and the werewolf?* The more the better. By the time it reaches you the werewolf should be in small, manageable chunks.

5. *Do I have a clear shot at it with my crossbow and silver bullets?* Hiding in the lavatory is not a good look. Try to find somewhere you can fire a few shots without putting yourself in any real danger.

6. *If I am using a screaming young person as bait, will he/she be safe?* [11]

[10] If battling in a large stately home, sitting in a chandelier high above the werewolf is ideal.
[11] Don't worry about this too much. Sometimes sacrifices must be made.

83

Growley Hall (West Wing Ground Floor)

Library

Study

Butler's Pantry

Hall

Stairs to First Floor

Dining Room

Key

Route of Werewolf
Route of Slayer
Bear Traps
Falling Net
Locked
Combat Area

Emergency Escape Route
Bait Trail
Caltrops
Crossbows
Tripwire
First Aid and Bandages

Exploding Chicken
Swinging Axe Trap
Chandelier
Assorted Weapons
Slaying Bone

Lures and Bait

It is far, far better to bring the werewolf to you than to chase it across town and country (which is **tiring**, **chilly**, **mucky** and **time-consuming**). Leave a trail of meat that leads to your clever trap *(tip: don't use live chickens - werewolves love them, but the chickens tend to wander off)* or - for even better results - use a **terrified** young lady wearing only her nightdress.[12] This is both traditional and effective. Try to choose someone who looks tender and juicy, and who screams well. Werewolves love a **screaming** victim.

If you cannot find a butcher's shop, or anyone idiotic enough to act as werewolf bait, try howling like a werewolf instead. Werewolves **protect** their territory fiercely and will **kill** any other werewolf muscling in. **A** good howl will have them bounding straight into your trap.

[12] A handsome young man wearing a vest can be substituted if you are dealing with a *female* werewolf, as long as he is screaming.

Up Close and Personal

If you have planned well, you should not need to fight the werewolf hand to claw. Nevertheless, if you have an audience, they will expect a little close **combat**. Try to put on a show - leaping on tables and swinging from chandeliers always gets a few "oohs" and "aaahs". For a successful slay, remember the following. . .

Keep your weapons in good working order. If your sword won't cut through butter the chances are it won't cut through a werewolf either.

Don't be afraid to use any items that happen to be laying around: chairs, tables and **priceless** antique vases; blazing logs from the fire; ornamental china kittens - most things can be used as a **weapon**. Try to use heavy/hard items - poking a werewolf to death with a soft cushion can be time-consuming.

A Trick Up Your Sleeve

Even the best plans sometimes go wrong, so never, never, never battle a werewolf without having a fallback option. For example, a few years ago I was fighting a particularly large and fearsome beast. One by one it survived all my traps. It had a dozen crossbow bolts sticking out of it and **bled** from a hundred wounds. Still, the beast attacked, roaring in triumph as it fell on me, its teeth **gnashing** and its claws ripping at my trousers.

Things did not
look good.

Fortunately, I was wearing
the Van Helsing Slayer Supplies
and Equipment Company's "Gentleman's
Stunner". I zapped the werewolf like a poodle
in a lightning storm and once again I, the great
Professor Van Helsing, won the day.

STRENGTHS AND WEAKNESSES

Yes, the werewolf is big and bad enough to make even the bravest person go running to Mummy. But, however strong the werewolf might be, it will have **weaknesses** too. The intelligent slayer aims to overcome the beast's strengths while taking full advantage of the chinks in its armour. (Note: not actual armour. If you see a werewolf wearing armour – run!)

STRENGTHS

TEETH

In a word: nasty. Keep clear of these or - even better - get rid of them. With the Van Helsing Slayer Supplies and Equipment Company's "Silver Jaw Breaker" boxing glove (or even just a large hammer), the slayer can make sure the werewolf will be eating its next meal through a straw.

CLAWS

It is difficult to de-claw a werewolf during a fight, and you would probably ruin your nail clippers. Don't even try. Instead, simply chop the beast's paw off with a sharp sword or axe. You'll no longer have to worry about claws, and the werewolf will be seriously cheesed off. [13]

EARS

Extremely sensitive. This can be turned to your advantage, however. Set off a loud siren, [14] and watch your deafened werewolf squeal.

EYES

The werewolf has extremely good eyesight so a poke in the eye should be one of the slayer's favourite tricks. The effects are immediate and spectacular. A blind werewolf is an easy-to-slay werewolf. Don't forget to swirl your finger around a bit!

WEAKNESSES

HEART

It's the bullseye of werewolf slaying. No living creature can shrug off a crossbow bolt to the heart.

BRAIN

The werewolf is a fiercely intelligent beast but will be unable to think clearly with a silver bullet rattling around in its head.

WOLFSBANE

Werewolves are immune to most poisons, except wolfsbane, which will melt them from the inside out until all that is left is a stinking pool of bubbling green goo. Very entertaining. The attractive plant with its dazzling blue flowers is easy to grow. Boil up a few and use it on the tips of arrows and crossbow bolts, or fry a steak in it and leave it out for your werewolf to discover.[15]

---

[13] With no paws, the werewolf will be slipping about like a camel on an ice rink and be much less likely to escape.

[14] Such as the Van Helsing Ear Splitter (only £24.99 - a snip).

[15] Wolfsbane also looks lovely in any flower arrangement and just the smell will keep werewolves away.

THE PACK

The last words of my dear old great-grandfather, Leopold Van Helsing, were, "Oh dear, I didn't know they came in packs, **aaaargghhhh...!**" Werewolves usually hunt alone but not always. There are few things as scary as a whole pack of werewolves bounding towards you, their great jaws hanging open and hunger burning in their eyes. At times like these you'll be glad you're wearing the **Van Helsing Slayer Supplies and Equipment Company's** ever-popular Rubber Knickers (guaranteed leakproof).

If you encounter a pack, you should either find a way to slay them one by one or collect your equipment and tiptoe away. For anyone ~~stupid~~ brave enough to face them all at once, my advice is this:

1 Every pack has a leader, known as the **alpha** werewolf. this will usually be the **biggest** and strongest. slaying this werewolf might make the others think twice before tangling with you. **Or it might not** - you will soon find out. **One** good shot and the rest may turn tail and flee. Either that or you will be almost instantly buried beneath a pile of snarling, hungry hell beasts. Good luck with that.

2 Run. Run as fast as you can. **Do not stop.** Do not turn around. **Scream** if you want to. It won't make any difference but it might make you feel a little better for two or three seconds until the pack runs you down.

Chapter 6

How to Slay a Werewolf

And so we come to the most **important** part of your journey: slaying. I hope you have learned your lessons well, young slayer. You will need everything I have taught you, plus nerves of steel and sturdy trousers. Remember: there is nothing to fear except fear itself (and a dirty great brute with teeth that could snap a lamp post in two). As the werewolf comes at you through the dark, its eyes glowing and its filthy breath shrivelling your eyebrows, stay calm, stop your knees from knocking and give it a wink. **YOU** are a slayer, and a slayer tweaks the nose of fear and pinches the bottom of death.

You will need one other thing – something that no book can teach: sharp wits. Successful slayers always stay one step ahead of their prey. Perhaps the best way to demonstrate is with one of my own cases:

VAN HELSING VERSUS THE BEAST OF WRIGGLESWORTH MOOR.

It started with a **letter**…

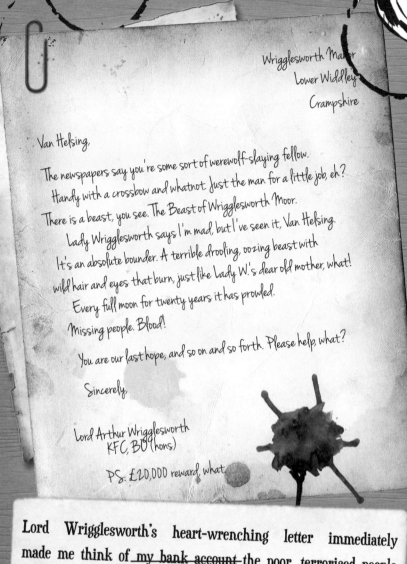

Wrigglesworth Manor
Lower Widdley
Crampshire

Van Helsing,

The newspapers say you're some sort of werewolf-slaying fellow.
Handy with a crossbow and whatnot. Just the man for a little job, eh?
There is a beast, you see. The Beast of Wrigglesworth Moor.
Lady Wrigglesworth says I'm mad, but I've seen it, Van Helsing.
It's an absolute bounder. A terrible drooling, oozing beast with
wild hair and eyes that burn, just like Lady W.'s dear old mother, what!
Every full moon for twenty years it has prowled.
Missing people. Blood!

You are our last hope, and so on and so forth. Please help, what?

Sincerely,

Lord Arthur Wrigglesworth
KFC, BO (hons)

PS: £20,000 reward, what

Lord Wrigglesworth's heart-wrenching letter immediately
made me think of ~~my bank account~~ the poor, terrorised people
of Lower Widdley. Only the great Van Helsing could release
them from their nightmare. Quickly, I dashed off a reply to
Lord Wrigglesworth in my own top-secret,
unbreakable code.

My dear Lord Wrigglesworth,

I am cabbage. Spank no one. Seaweed is of the
utmost irrelevance.
I will confuse you when my invertibrations are ham.

Love,

I checked the calendar. The next full moon was the
following night. Quickly, I packed weapons, traps and slaying
clothes. Disguised as Jeremy Poot, an inspector of drains, I
caught the train to Crampshire that very afternoon.

The train arrived at sunset. At first sight, Lower Widdley seemed a neat village of thatched cottages and
cheese shops. But I found there was no jewellery shop
(no silver!) and every house had iron bars on the windows.
It reminded me of Grüselighausen. An old inn - the Dog and
Crumpet - stood on a wide green. I entered, already alert for signs
of werewolves.

Inside, the inn was dark, lit only by a few dripping candles.
Behind the bar a grizzled-looking fellow with pointed ears,
hairy knuckles and eyebrows that met in the middle was
scratching his head. "Excuse me, sir," he said. "Touch of
the fleas."

A-ha! I thought to myself. *I shall need to keep a close eye on this chap...*

"Top of the evening to you, my good man," I said aloud. "Do you have a room available? I am Jeremy Poot, Her Majesty's Inspector of Drains. I shall be staying in your charming village for a few days while I inspect the...aaah... drains." Quietly, I added, "Woof woof," just to see what he would make of it.

"If you don't mind, sir, I'm a happily married man," he replied with a sniff. "Room 3 is available." Turning, he cried out, "Mrs *Buuuuuurbage.*"

A hunched old woman appeared. Hair sprouted from her ears. She snuffled as she walked towards me and I leaned back – the stench of her breath could have peeled paint from the walls.

"My wife, the lovely **Mrs Burbage**," the innkeeper explained. "She'll take your bags."

I stared, aghast, as Mrs Burbage shuffled away. Could I have found not one but *two* werewolves so quickly?

Shaken, I ordered a pint of the local ale - **Vicar's Armpit**, I think it was called - and looked around the inn.

My jaw dropped open.

Sitting at a table was a woman with a large beard talking to a man so hairy that only his eyes could be seen through the thick mat of fur on his head. **A** fellow with sharp, yellow fingernails tore at a raw steak with his teeth. Everywhere I looked, there were hair and ears and twitching noses and enormous eyebrows. My gaze rested on a petite, red-haired woman with the smoothest, softest skin I had ever seen. "**Who** is that?" I asked the innkeeper.

"**Miss Larkin**, the geography teacher. **A *strange* woman.**"

I shook my head. What kind of topsy-turvy village was **Lower Widdley** where only the geography teacher - usually the hairiest of people - looked normal? Were the villagers one huge pack of werewolves? My slayer senses told me to run, but I kept cool. "Mr Burbage," I said, "I'm short of pound notes. May I pay with these **silver coins?**"

He grabbed them from my hand with a "Thank ee kindly, sir," and bit one to make sure it was real.

Once again, my jaw dropped. A werewolf would rather put a wasps' nest in its mouth than silver. Clearly, it was going to be tricky to find the werewolf of Lower Widdley. From what I had already seen, it could be any one of several dozen people. "Do you have a local newspaper?" I asked, thinking I might find some clues there.

I took a slurp of Vicar's Armpit as I read. But there was no sign of the mysterious disappearances Lord Wrigglesworth had told me about. The front page of the Lower Widdley Gazette told me that Mr Crowther of Dump Street had been attacked by ducks while fishing in the local pond, and Mrs Gertrude Ulcer had won the Annual Toad Bake for the third year in a row. I tossed it away.

"Oi!" said a voice from the darkness at the back of the pub. "You ain't no drains inspector. You're that bloke from the papers. That nutty Professor Van Helspring – the slayer."

Silence fell like a very quiet hammer. A sea of hairy faces scowled at me.

Drat, I thought to myself. *So much for disguises.* I decided I would have to be honest. "Yes, you're right," I declared, throwing aside my wig and glasses. "Jeremy Poot was just a disguise. In fact, I am the great Professor Van Helsing, come to rid you of the werewolf curse."

"**Shhh!** We don't talk of such things, Mr Poot," hissed Burbage, who seemed a little slow to catch on. "It's **dangerous**."

"More than our lives are worth, talking to the likes of him," said Mrs Burbage.

"And there's no point talking, anyway," said Burbage. "It's a full moon tomorrow. If you've come a-hunting the beast-that-is-not-named, Mr Poot, you'll be dead by midnight. Enjoy the taste of the Vicar's Armpit while you still can!"

I went to bed with a sick feeling in my stomach, and not just from the ale. The next day was no better – my enquiries were just as fruitless as the night before. News of my mission had spread. No one would speak to me. Most of the villagers scuttled away when they saw me coming. There was only one way I was going to find this beast.

I would have to track it.

As the sun disappeared below the horizon through the barred window of dingy Room 3, I slipped into my third-best slayer outfit: thick, silver-stitched underwear, a suit of midnight black with a heavy leather coat, silver rings and a wide-brimmed hat. I added a woolly scarf and tucked some mittens into my pocket. It looked like it would be a chilly night.

When tracking, speed is essential, so I picked my weapons with care: a large crossbow that I slung over my back, a sword, caltrops, four knives and three daggers, two silver-bullet pistols and a set of Transylvanian Wolf Clamps. Plus, of course, an Exploding Chicken. I added a pair of night-sight binoculars and my Detect-o-Wolf hearing apparatus. And a jam sandwich.

100

I was ready.

As I left the inn, with a nod to the silent customers, village doors and shutters banged shut around me. A full moon was already climbing the sky. All I had to do was find the werewolf and slay it. Or I could catch the train home and put my feet up by the fire. The **10.17 pm** to London was due at any moment.

It was tempting, but a **Van Helsing** (almost) *never* runs away from a werewolf. Not until it's absolutely necessary, at least (or sometimes because I suddenly remember I have an urgent appointment at the hairdresser). **Shaking** my head, I vaulted over a fence and rolled around in muck to disguise my smell. I smiled as I rubbed a cowpat into my face.

Once again, **Van Helsing** was on the hunt.

101

The moon shone down as I ran across the moor. Keeping to the shadows, I stopped here and there, listening through the **Van Helsing Detect-o-Wolf** and scanning the horizon with my binoculars.

Nothing.

The werewolf was out there though. It *had* to be.

At exactly midnight an unmistakable howl drifted across the moor: **Arr-oooooooooooo**. Quickly, I made my way towards it and soon picked up the werewolf's prints - it looked to be a *huge* beast. Its head would make a marvellous footstool for my sitting room.

Arr-oooooooooooooooooooooooooo.

The howl was louder now. I noticed a sign for **Creaking Bottom** Farm. So that was where the **beast** was heading!

I arrived just in time. A massive werewolf stood hunched in the farmyard, its teeth around the ankle of a young man. He **screamed** as the beast dragged him across the cobbles.

I took my crossbow and silently slipped a bolt in. A light breeze caught my coat, flapping it out as I stood **silhouetted** against the full moon. If my face hadn't been smeared with cowpat I would have looked *extremely* nifty. Still, there was nothing I could do about that. No one ever said being a slayer is easy.

I clicked the safety catch off the crossbow. The werewolf's ears **pricked** up instantly. Dropping the young farmer, who curled up on the cobbled ground, it turned to face me. A snarl appeared on its hideous face, its teeth dripping in the moonlight. **Bloodshot eyes** glared at me through matted, greasy fur.

"Hello, pretty," I said, quietly. "I *love* what you've done with your hair."

For a second the beast looked shocked. It had probably never seen a human who wasn't screaming before.

The look passed in a moment. Roaring in fury, the werewolf sprang at me.

I fired the **crossbow.**

The beast dodged. It was fast – too fast. I gulped. There was no time for traps and gizmos. I had to think quickly…

But the werewolf was already upon me, its foul breath in my face as it knocked me to the ground. A mountain of stinking fur and muscle held me pinned on the cold stone.

It snarled. Its jaws opened.

Drool dripped.

It was all quite awful.

I was certain I was dead.

Then I heard a shout:

"Gerroff him, you **'orrible** great **twazzock!"**

A heavy boot landed on the side of the beast's head, and a flaming torch was thrust in its face. The farmer! The werewolf reared back, freeing one of my arms. I punched it on the nose with a fistful of silver rings and sprang to my feet as it howled in pain and scrabbled backwards.

Drawing my sword, I said, "This is a **Van Helsing Slayer Supplies and Equipment Company Number Three Broadsword – the WolfSlicer.** It is razor sharp and plated with silver. Also, I have an Exploding Chicken in my pocket."

The werewolf looked from me to the farmer and back again. It snarled again, baring its **razor-sharp teeth**. Then it stopped, lifted its hairy ears and bounded away. In a second it was gone.

Looking down, I saw that the werewolf's claws had shredded my third-best trousers. I scowled. The great Van Helsing would have his revenge. In the meantime, I took a map from my pocket and studied the direction in which it had fled.

"You're that **mad professor** what everyone's whispering about," interrupted the farmer. "You saved my life. How can I ever repay you?"

I handed him
my card.

PROFESSOR VAN HELSING

TEL: LONDON 56773

WEREWOLVES SLAIN. LIVES SAVED.
REWARDS ACCEPTED.

PLEASE NOTE THAT I AM **NOT** MAD.

"I don't have nothing to reward you with, professor, sir," said the farmer. "Unless you likes turnips. I got lots of turnips."

"Keep your turnips," I said, looking up from the map. "Perhaps, instead, you could do me a **favour**…"

"So, the beast got away, did it?" mumbled Lord Wrigglesworth the next afternoon. "Bad show, what."

We were standing in the entrance hall of Wrigglesworth Manor, a fine old house of turrets and red brick. His Lordship was a tall, grey fellow with a drooping moustache, a drooping nose and drooping eyes. "This time it escaped me, my lord," I admitted. "But there is another full moon this evening. Tonight it won't be so lucky, not with the trap I have planned."

"Good man, Van Helsing. Where?"

I looked around the entrance hall. It had a main door of thick oak and iron. The windows were too small for any werewolf, but would provide excellent escape routes for a medium-sized slayer. Perfect. "Here, if you please, my lord. And I will need bait."

"Meat, what," replied Lord Wrigglesworth.

"A screaming young woman is *traditional*, my lord."

At that moment **Lady Wrigglesworth** reappeared. A tall woman with a face like a pickaxe, she had been staring at me with disgust all morning. She cleared her throat and looked over the top of her spectacles. "You may use our daughter," she said.

Lord Wrigglesworth started. "*Lucy?*" he gurgled. "My own, sweet *Lucy*? Are you sure, my dear?"

"Since I don't believe a word of this silly werewolf nonsense, what is the worst that could happen?" Lady W. sniffed.

"Well, she could be eaten, what," muttered Lord Wrigglesworth.

"**Stuff** and **nonsense**," sneered Lady W. "Even if werewolves do exist, I'm sure Lucy will be perfectly safe with the professor."

For the remainder of the day, I prepared the manor. I spread **silver caltrops** around the main entrance and fitted the doors with springs to prevent the werewolf from escaping. Tripwires lay across the floor.

"My daughter, Lucy," said Lord Wrigglesworth as I finished laying my traps. I turned around - on his arm was a young woman with curly blonde hair. "You *will* take care of her, won't you, Van Helsing, what?"

"Oh yes, my lord," I told him, raising an eyebrow. "You can be certain of that."

Turning to Lucy, I explained her part in the plan. She would scream to attract the werewolf's attention and the beast would bound through the doors and make straight for her, setting off every trap, while I fired from the top of the stairs with a crossbow and pistols. "It will be dead before it's halfway across the room," I said confidently.

"How exciting," giggled Lucy, clapping her hands together.

"Too exciting for me, I'm sure," Lady W. interrupted with a sniff of contempt. "I shall take an early night. One of my headaches is coming on."

Together, Lord Wrigglesworth and I enjoyed a dinner of roast pheasant and a pint of Grandad's Bathwater. Then he retired to the shed to watch through a pair of binoculars.

All was ready. It was time to slay a werewolf.

Slowly, a full moon rose over Wrigglesworth Manor. I took my position at the top of the stairs - well out of harm's way - and nodded towards Lucy. She filled her lungs and let out an ear-splitting shriek. "Excellent," I told her. "And again if you please, young lady."

It wasn't long before I heard an A₁₁-ooooooooo from across the moor. The wolf was soon at the door - its great shadow fell across the hallway. A second later, it crept into Wrigglesworth Manor, snarling.

BOOM. The door slammed shut behind it, shaking the manor's ancient stones.

"Oh my, what big teeth you have," screamed Lucy, clasping her hands together in girlish fear.

The werewolf bounded across the hall, setting off my traps. Metal jaws clanged shut and crossbow bolts zipped and zinged across the room, breaking a number of valuable vases that I had forgotten to remove.

But something was wrong. The werewolf had neatly avoided every trap. And it wasn't pouncing at the beautiful and very appetising Lucy. It was bounding towards...

ME!

The farmer had done his job well. The villagers of Lower Widdley wouldn't trust a stranger but they would trust him - one of their own. Lady Wrigglesworth and her daughter would never escape the fire started by the villagers' torches.

So, your little werewolf problem has been solved, Lord Wrigglesworth. Is it a bad time to talk about that reward?

And that, young slayer, is how to slay a werewolf.

Professor
Van Helsing Phd BA Dip GNVQ
BSC PGCE HND BE BEC CBic
BDA BSM CD CGEO

Chapter 7
LAST WORDS

"Professor Van Helsing," I hear you say. "You are an amazing teacher. Totally awesome."

I know, young slayer, but hold on just one moment. If you have learned your lessons well and trained hard, the very sight of you will strike fear into the ghastly, ravenous heart of every werewolf. Nevertheless, while every slayer needs a confident swagger (as well as the ability to flick bogies in the face of certain death), a slayer who is *too* confident is a slayer who is destined to find out what a werewolf looks like from the inside. Before you steal out into the night, as quiet as a shadow, as deadly as a year-old ham sandwich, there are still a few things you should know...

THE CHECKLIST

An essential part of your preparations, the checklist should be completed before every slaying. Even a first-class brain like mine sometimes forgets **important details,** and the last thing you want to be doing as a werewolf leaps at you with moonlight glinting off its dripping fangs is to be rummaging around for that pistol you're *sure* you packed. Make a checklist and tick off *everything* before attempting to slay. It should look something like this...

CHECKLIST

☐ **A**re all my gizmos packed and my weapons sharp, ready to use and in the right pockets? [16]

☐ **H**ave I abstained from beans and cabbage for at least twenty-four hours? Silence is often key to survival – do not be betrayed by your own bottom.

☐ **I**s my hair styled and my outfit looking snazzy? **A** slayer without style is just a scruff with a crossbow.

☐ **D**o I have a plan and back-up plans? You will have to think on your feet, but do **NOT** try making up plans as you go. Slayers often lose concentration when a werewolf is trying to pull their ears off.

☐ **A**re all my traps laid and tested? (Be careful with this – slaying is *much* more difficult if you are hanging upside down by one ankle in your own trap.)

☐ **I**s the moon full? It is surprising how many slayers forget to check. Spending all night squatting in a bush or twiddling your thumbs in a carefully prepared trap is both dull and embarrassing.

[16] I once tried to pull a dagger from my pocket only to find that I had packed a cheese sandwich by mistake. Luckily, the cheese was extremely sharp.

WHEN SLAYING GOES WRONG

Had an off day? Slaying not gone quite to plan? If so, you'll probably be dead by now (in which case you need not read the rest of this section). However, you may just be lucky and only lose an arm or a leg or two. Don't be downhearted – every slayer collects a few scars along the way and they make for great stories to share with other slayers. Check out my own on the right...

If things do go wrong, the most important advice to remember is: **DON'T PANIC!** Keep a cool head (even if it's in a werewolf's mouth) and you might still make it out alive. If you have a weapon within reach, then what are you waiting for? Either get on with it or sprinkle some salt and pepper on yourself. If not, you can try poking it in the eye or biting it on the nose but a werewolf drooling over its next meal is not easy to distract. At times like these you need **Van Helsing's Last Resort.**

BULLET WOUND IN SHOULDER

This is where a screaming young lady shot me by mistake while I was wrestling a werewolf. (Note: never give your bait weapons unless they have had their eyesight fully checked.)

MISSING EARLOBE

I lost my earlobe to a Kitsune during a struggle in a Chinese restaurant. The cheeky devil dipped it in soy sauce and swallowed it whole.

CLAW MARKS DOWN CHEST

I collected this scar during some rough-and-tumble with a Mexican Nagual that surprised me in the bath. I eventually choked it to death by shoving a rubber duck down its throat.

LARGE SCAR DOWN ARM

This scar was given to me by Herman Schnausermann all those years ago in Grüselighausen. It reminds me never to underestimate the evil of werewolves, or bank managers.

LARGE BITE MARK ON LEG

This beauty was given to me by a werewolf in Sweden. The beast wasn't quite as dead as I thought it was as I tested it out as a new fireside rug.

NEXT STEPS FOR THE SUCCESSFUL SLAYER

Don't fear, dear reader - after following the steps in this book it is highly likely you will be **victorious**. The werewolf will lie dead at your feet and, thanks to you, the world is a safer place. Hurrah for you (and for me, because I trained you). But what next? A nice, hot bubble bath before collecting your reward and facing the cheering crowd? No, young slayer - your job is not yet finished. You can't just leave a dead werewolf lying around the place.

"Hang on there, Van," **you say.** "I've done all the hard work, can't someone else bury the revolting thing?"

But wait: don't bury it. That would be a waste. A *live* werewolf is an ugly brute but a *dead* werewolf can be both attractive and useful. And after trying to tear you limb from limb, the least the beast can do is help decorate your home. Werewolf skin makes luxurious rugs and cushions, and its fur can also provide delightfully warm hats, coats and gloves, but use your imagination - almost every part of a werewolf can be used (be sure to wash it thoroughly in hot, soapy water first). Here are just a few ideas...

THE COAT RACK

A stuffed werewolf by the front door makes an excellent place to hang your coat and is sure to impress your guests.

THE REMOTE-CONTROL WEREWOLF BUTLER

Slayers who like pottering around in the gadget laboratory may wish to use a few gizmos to create their own wolfy butler. Not only will your guests be thrilled when served tea by a "real" werewolf but the remote-control werewolf butler is guaranteed to get rid of door-to-door salesmen, rent collectors, annoying people from the tax office and anyone else you'd rather not speak to.

121

THE MOUNTED HEAD

A design classic, the mounted werewolf head makes an excellent souvenir of your hunt and adds a note of elegance to any room (except the toilet - the sudden sight of a snarling werewolf head can lead guests to having little "accidents").

KEY HOOK

Tired of losing your keys? That's not likely to happen again if your key hook is made from a handsome, stuffed werewolf paw. These can also be used as toast or letter racks, combs, salad tongs and even attractive hairclips.

BACK SCRUBBER

The werewolf's tail is long and bristly - perfect for cleaning those hard-to-reach places at bath time!

BOOKMARK

Even a werewolf's ear can be useful! And every time you open your current bedtime reading (I recommend *Why I Am Fabulous* by Prof. V. Helsing), you'll be reminded of your glorious victory.

FAREWELL, AND HAPPY SLAYING

Congratulations, young slayer, you are ready to prowl the night in search of your first werewolf. Be warned: there will be people who call you mad. They will laugh and jeer and poke fun at you. Ignore them (or kick them up the bottom if you prefer). It doesn't matter. We know better. *We* know that the rewards of exterminating these diabolical vermin are enormous.

Firstly, you will have all the fur underwear anyone could dream of. Secondly, beast by drooling beast we are pushing back the dark tide of Evil and all that. Thirdly, and most importantly, there are the *actual* rewards - the standard rate is £10,000 per werewolf plus expenses.[17]

Farewell for now, young slayer. Wherever you hunt, I wish you many moonlight adventures and leave you with one last piece of advice: if at first you don't succeed then you'll be eaten, in which case slaying is probably not for you. Still, you can rest assured that if you *do* become a werewolf's dinner, Professor Van Helsing will give you a full refund for the price of this book.
All you have to do is apply in person.

Happy slaying.

[17] People will try to knock the price down, I show my scars and tell them that if they don't want to offer the proper reward they can always slay the werewolf themselves. It's amazing how quickly they get their wallets out.